BULLFROG
AND GERTRUDE
GO CAMPING

BULLFROG AND GERTRUDE GO CAMPING

BY ROSAMOND DAUER
ILLUSTRATED BY BYRON BARTON

A Young Yearling Book

Published by
Dell Publishing
a division of
Bantam Doubleday Dell Publishing Group, Inc.
666 Fifth Avenue
New York, New York 10103

ISBN: 0-440-40074-0

Reprinted by arrangement with William Morrow and Company, Inc. on behalf of Greenwillow Books

Printed in the United States of America

August 1988

10 9 8 7 6 5 4 3

WES

For my sister Anne

"Let's go camping!"
Bullfrog said
to Gertrude one morning.
"Oh, I'd like that,"
Gertrude said.

So they packed
and set out for the big woods.

"Ah," said Bullfrog
    as they traveled,
"walking is good for us!"
"Why, yes," Gertrude said,
    panting up a steep hill.

When they entered a clearing,

Bullfrog said,

"I think I've had enough walking."

"Fine," said Gertrude.

"I'll get some wood."

"How would you like
blueberry muffins for dinner?"
asked Bullfrog.

"My favorite!" Gertrude said,
and she went into the woods.

Just when Gertrude

had her arms full of sticks,

she heard a strange sound.

PSSSSSSSST!

Gertrude turned quickly
and dropped her wood.
"What's that?" she said.

A voice said, "Here I am!"

Gertrude looked down.

"It's a snake!" she cried.

"Itsa Snake,"

  said a very small snake.

"Wonderful.

  You've given me my name."

"What?" asked Gertrude.

"My name is Itsa Snake,

  and I'm harmless."

"Oh," Gertrude said.

"In that case,

  how do you do?"

"As a matter of fact,"
Itsa said, "I'm lonesome.
May I stay with you?"
"Well," said Gertrude,
picking up her wood,
"you could come back with me
and have some dinner."

"Oh, thank you!"

Itsa said.

And Itsa followed Gertrude

back to the clearing.

When Bullfrog saw Gertrude,

he shouted,

"Just in time for dinner!"

Then he stopped.

He pointed to the snake

and said, "Who's that?"

"Itsa Snake," Gertrude said.

"That I can see," said Bullfrog.

"Itsa is my name,"
  said the snake,

"and I'm harmless."

"Thank goodness!"
  Bullfrog said.

"Let's have dinner,"
suggested Gertrude.
Bullfrog looked at Itsa.
"Do you like blueberry muffins?"
"Oh, yes!" said Itsa.
"That's good," Bullfrog said.
"You seem to be a smart snake."

The three of them
had a delicious dinner.

Soon it was time for bed.
Gertrude got into
her sleeping bag.
Bullfrog got into
his sleeping bag.

And Itsa Snake

tried to get into

Bullfrog's sleeping bag.

"No! No!" said Bullfrog,

   picking up Itsa

   and putting her on the ground.

"You must stay out!"

   He pointed at Itsa.

"Sit!" he said.

"My dear Bullfrog,"

Gertrude said sleepily,

"I believe you should say 'Coil!' "

"You're right," Bullfrog said.

"Coil, Itsa!"

Itsa coiled up next to Bullfrog.

The next morning,
Bullfrog woke up
to find Itsa
on top of his sleeping bag
and flicking her tongue
in and out.
"Don't stick your tongue out
at me!" said Bullfrog,
getting up.

"I beg your pardon,"
  said Itsa.
"I got carried away."
  Gertrude was fixing breakfast.
"Time to eat!" she called.

After breakfast,

Bullfrog put out the fire.

Gertrude said,

"I think I'll pick

some of these shiny leaves

and take them home."

But Itsa cried,

"Stop! Don't pick them!"

"And why not?" asked Bullfrog.

"Because," said Itsa,

"that's poison ivy."

"Imagine a harmless snake
knowing about poison ivy,"
Bullfrog said.

"Oh, thank you, Itsa,"

said Gertrude.

"What a helpful snake you are!"

"I could be helpful

about other things, too,"

Itsa offered.

"I'm sure you could,"
said Bullfrog,
"but I'm afraid
we must be leaving."

"Well, it was nice
to meet you,"
Itsa said sadly.
And Bullfrog and Gertrude
started to walk home.

After a short time

Gertrude said,

"You don't suppose…?"

"No!" Bullfrog said.

"But, Bullfrog," Gertrude said,

"you were adopted

by the Mouse family."

"I know," said Bullfrog.

"But I was

a very good-looking tadpole."

"I see," said Gertrude,

and they walked on in silence.

Bullfrog soon stopped.

"On the other hand,"

he said,

"Itsa isn't bad-looking

for a snake.

And perhaps she could be useful."

"What do you mean?"

asked Gertrude.

"Oh, maybe Itsa could help me
  measure things," Bullfrog said.
"Do you think,"
  Gertrude asked,
"Itsa is a snake we could love?"
  Bullfrog thought a minute.
"Yes," he said.
"But I wonder if
  she knows how to play cards."

"We could teach her!"

Gertrude said.

"Hmmmmm...," said Bullfrog.

"Do you think we...?"

"Yes!" Gertrude said.

"Very well," said Bullfrog.

He turned around.

"Itsa! Itsa Snake!"

he called.

Soon they could see Itsa Snake
bouncing down the path
toward them.

"You have made me very happy,"

Itsa said

when she caught up to them.

So the three of them
went home and talked about
all the things
they would do as a family.